DAVID ALMOND

PAPER BOAT, PAPER BIRD

Illustrated by Kirsti Beautyman

HODDER

PAPER BOAT, PAPER BIRD

Other books by David Almond

Skellig

My Name is Mina

Kit's Wilderness

Heaven Eyes

Counting Stars

Secret Heart

The Fire Eaters

Clay

Jackdaw Summer

Wild Girl, Wild Boy – A Play

Skellig – A Play

A Song for Ella Grey

The Colour of the Sun

Bone Music

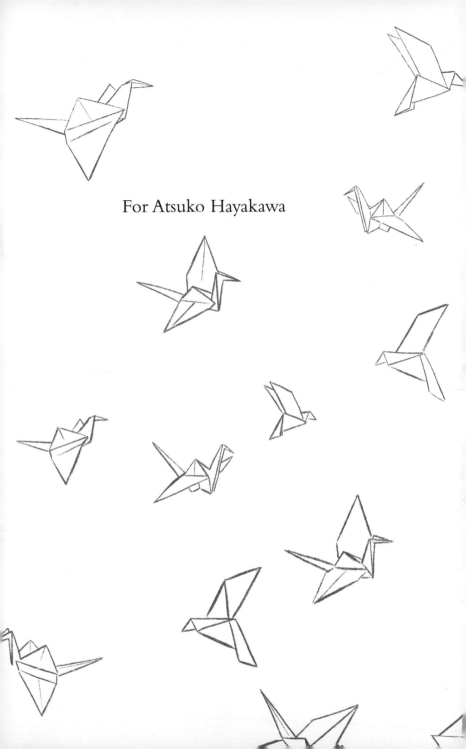

For Atsuko Hayakawa

HODDER CHILDREN'S BOOKS
First published in Great Britain in 2022 by Hodder & Stoughton

1 3 5 7 9 10 8 6 4 2

Text copyright © David Almond, 2022
Illustrations © Kirsti Beautyman 2022

A CIP catalogue record for this book is available from the British Library.

HB ISBN 978 1 444 96327 4

PB ISBN 978 1 444 96328 1

Printed and bound in China

The paper and board used in this book
are made from wood from responsible sources.

Hodder Children's Books
An imprint of Hachette Children's Group
Part of Hodder & Stoughton Limited
Carmelite House
50 Victoria Embankment
London EC4Y 0DZ

An Hachette UK Company
www.hachette.co.uk

www.hachettechildrens.co.uk

Kyoto. Kee-oh-toe! She feels so weirdly at home. She is herself, Mina, but it's like there's another Mina waiting to be discovered or created here.

"That's travel," says her mum. "Turns the world into somewhere else and turns you into someone else."

This morning they're off to the Golden Temple. They're on a packed bus. Mina stands squashed in the aisle. Her mum's watching for the temple stop. She keeps turning and peering through the bodies. Mina waves: don't worry. Look! Here I am!

There's a woman sitting on a seat beside her. The woman appears to be completely on her own. She's calmly folding a square sheet of paper.

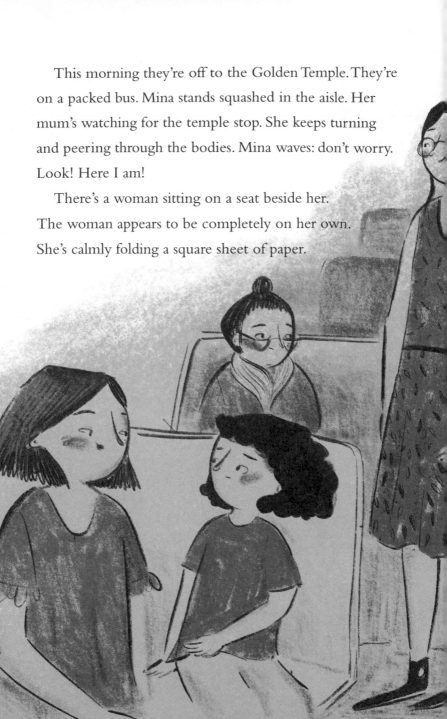

She folds it edge to edge, point to point. She opens it, closes it, tugs and teases it into shape. Her lips move, as if she's silently singing in time with the movement of her fingers. She swiftly makes a little boat. She holds it on her open palm and moves her hand gently back and forward, up and down. It's like she's on the bus but not on the bus. The boat moves as if it's floating on a lake inside the bus that's there for anyone to know.

She sees Mina watching. She smiles and bows her head.

"Konnichiwa," she says.

Mina smiles and bows her head as well.

"Konnichiwa."

She feels the strange neat movements of her lips and throat and tongue as they make the lovely word. She says it again to feel the word in her mouth and to hear the sharp sound of it.

"Kon-ni-chi-wa."

The woman floats the boat towards Mina with her hands.

Go on, take it, she says with her eyes.

Mina takes it and rests it on her own palm.

"Arigato," she says. "A-ri-ga-to."

Float it, says the woman with her eyes.

Mina floats it through the tiny empty spaces around her body and the spaces open and the waters rise.

The woman laughs and claps her hands silently. She starts on another sheet of paper – folds it, creases it, tugs and teases it into shape. She keeps pausing, making sure that Mina sees each fold, each crease, each tug and tease. Look, she's saying, this is how it's done. Mina watches the woman's fingers and the crowds around her disappear. Kyoto is gone.

The bus is gone. She imagines what it would be like to be a sheet of paper in the woman's hands, to be folded and creased and teased into shape, to become a paper Mina.

Maybe the woman knows this. She smiles deep into Mina's eyes as if she knows everything.

The paper in the woman's hand becomes a little sharp-winged sharp-beaked bird. She holds it between her thumb and fingers and flies it through the spaces around her. She flies it towards Mina.

Take it, she says with her eyes. Fly it.

"Arigato," says Mina.

She takes the bird. She can feel the vibrations of the woman's fingers within it. With the bird flying between her fingers, she's surrounded by empty air, by great stretches of water.

The bus sighs to a halt. The woman shrugs, smiles, stands up.

"Sayōnara," she says.

She hands Mina some sheets of paper.

"Sa-yō-na-ra," says Mina. "A-ri-ga-to."

The woman twists her way to the opening door and she steps out into the crowds.

Mina looks through her own reflection into the street outside. She sees the woman then loses sight of her then sees her again but the crowds close around her and the bus moves on and she's gone.

Mina carefully folds the boat and the bird flat and puts them into her sketchbook with the sheets of paper.

The bus continues through the busy streets, through all the noise, past skyscrapers, hotels, flower sellers, flashing lights, cyclists, geishas, sushi shops, punks, cinemas, statues, tourist groups, burger bars, lanterns, pachinko parlours, shrines, road signs, lorries, buses, cars, crowds.

Mina sees how beautiful it all is. So much of it is recognisable, but so much of it is just so strange. The bus glides and sways. The bodies around her sway against her. The thrill of being here in Kyoto! She remembers roaring up into the clouds and leaving England behind.

Then the oceans they crossed, the sky they flew through, the mountains and countries and cities below. Now home is on the Earth's far side and this is Japan. She saw it first at the crack of dawn from miles up in the sky. There it was, the country that seemed to float on the sea.

"Ja-pan," she whispers. "Kyo-to!"

She feels the little bursts of breath in her mouth. She thinks of the world turning and turning through endless space. She feels the great stretches of emptiness that are inside her.

"Mina!" calls her mum. "Mina, here we are!"

The bodies part, letting Mina through.

"Here I am," she says.

They walk along the path towards the temple gardens.

"Keep close," says her mum. "Don't get lost."

Mina shows her lovely paper gifts.

She floats the boat and flies the bird.

They buy their tickets, which bear the name of the place then a picture of it, then unreadable and beautiful writing beneath.

The gravel gently rattles under their feet as they walk through the gates. There are rocks, pine trees, narrow pathways, stone lanterns, then the lake, then the golden temple, and beyond the temple there are trees, low hills then dark and distant mountains and the sky.

"The temple's called Kinkaku-ji," says her mum.

"Kin-ka-ku-ji," says Mina.

"It contains the ashes of Buddha. It was burned down by a distressed monk in 1950 and was rebuilt again. It is considered to be the same place, even though it's new."

She sighs and laughs at the outrageous idea, at the outrageous beauty of the place.

"Maybe it suggests that nothing is ever truly lost, that everything will return."

"Maybe," says Mina.

She thinks of her lost dad for a few moments, as she does each day. He would have loved this place so much. Then she turns her mind back to the temple.

It is reflected in the lake. It appears to be floating on another temple. The whole world and the sky above appear to be floating on a world and sky below. Mina looks down into the lake, and another Mina looks back up at her.

"Konnichiwa," she whispers.

"Kon-ni-chi-wa," mouths the other Mina.

Now her mum looks back at her from the lake and waves. Mina sees how alike they are, how they are reflected in each other.

"Konnichiwa," they say.

Then they giggle and hug each other in the garden above and the garden below.

Mum goes wandering. Mina sits on a rock by the lake and watches all visitors. A man and boy crouch close by her and peer down into the water as if they're passionately searching for something. Many people do the same, of course, as if the glassy water pulls them to it. When the man and boy stand up, the boy pretends that he's about to dive in. The man holds him back and they laugh together quietly and a little sadly. Then they walk on.

She catches the boy's eye as he passes by.

"Konnichiwa," she whispers, but he's lost in thought.

Mina draws a picture of the temple. She speaks its name, Kinkaku-ji, as she draws, and she writes the name, too, so that the image, the word, the sound and its movements are all the same thing.

She writes a tiny note about what happened in the bus:

The packed Kyoto bus. A paper-folding woman.
Birds fly from her hands.

She takes a piece of the woman's paper and writes a message on it.

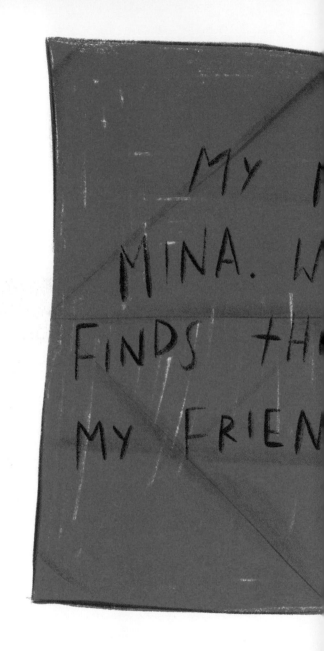

MY
MINA. W
FINDS THE
MY FRIEN

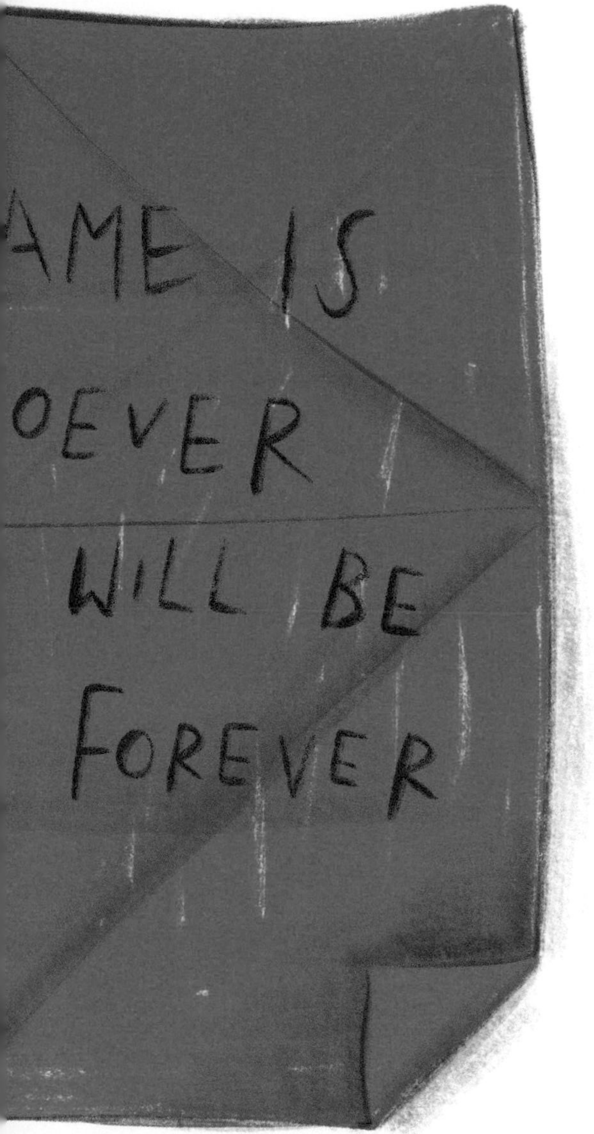

AME IS

OEVER

WILL BE

FOREVER

She folds the paper edge to edge, point to point. She makes a boat with it. Nowhere near as good as the woman's boat, but something the same. She takes another sheet of paper and folds that, too.

On this she simply writes, Mina.

She makes a bird with it, again nowhere near as good but still it's a bird.

She looks at the world, blinks, and looks again. She imagines a whole world made of folded paper: paper temple, paper trees, paper rocks, paper people, all neatly folded and creased in a paper world. She smiles at the lovely illusion.

Then she puts the bird into the boat and stands up.

There are streams flowing through the garden. She kneels beside one of them and carefully places the boat into it and lets it go.

"Sayōnara," she whispers as the boat and the bird are carried away through the rocks and the pine trees. "Sa-yō-na-ra," until they've completely gone from sight.

Then her mum's voice:

"Mina! Where are you?"

Mina hurries back to the lake. She waves.

"I'm here!" she calls.

"I'm here," she calls silently from the world below.

That evening they eat sushi and sashimi and flakes of something that's hardly there at all except for the intensity of the taste it leaves on the tongue. They walk home through the crowds past the blazing lights of bars and department stores. They're staying in a little timber house in a narrow street near the centre of the town. It's a place with small sparse rooms, low lights, pale gliding shutters, tatami mats on the floors. There's a bathroom with a deep stone bath.

In Mina's room a little stone
Buddha sits in a shrine with sprigs
of cherry blossom and an incense burner.
Mina lights the incense and scented smoke
drifts through the room. She puts her bird and
her boat on the shrine. She lies on a futon on
the floor. Her mum's singing in the room
next door. The city drones beyond the
walls. The moon shines in through
the window. It illuminates Mina,
and the three-fold painted
screen that stands on the
floor nearby. Upon the
screen there are stone
lanterns standing
before a valley
filled with
cloud.

There are distant jagged mountains. Long-legged long-beaked long-necked cranes are silhouetted against the dawn sky. They appear to be flying through this world towards another or into this world from another.

When she sleeps, she dreams of the bird and the boat that have been carried away, She dreams of being the paper-folding woman. She folds and creases and tugs and teases. She holds her creations in her open hands: look, this is how it's done. Deep into her dreams she makes a dark-haired dark-eyed boy.

The boy smiles.

Mina smiles back at him.

"Konnichiwa," she says.

Her lips and tongue and breath form the sharp neat shapes and sounds.

"Kon-ni-chi-wa."

And then she falls into the deep dark silent lake that surrounds us all.

Early next morning, at the edge of Kyoto, the boy is swimming in Biwa Lake. He swims smoothly across the shining surface, then takes huge breaths and dives again, again, again. He loves moving in the depths, with the light above and the darkness below and the silvery flashes of fish around him. He loves to burst out into the air, to curve, to dive down deep again.

This morning there isn't much time. His father's already called him.

"Miyako! Miyako!"

He climbs out on to the bank and crouches at the edge. He bangs two sticks together.

Crack! Crack! Crack!

Black and silver fish rise and gather at the sound.

Crack! Crack! Crack!

"Konnichiwa," he whispers.

He drops crumbs towards their mouths that
silently open and close, open and close.

"O O O," say the fish in silence. "O O O."

"Sayōnara," says Miyako.

He's turning away when a little paper boat
appears, floating on the surface. He leans
down and lifts it out. There's a paper bird inside it.

"Miyako!" calls his father. "We have to go!"

He stands and sees his father on the narrow beach beside their towels.

"Where are you, Miyako?"

"Look! I'm here, Dad!"

He hurries to him. He dries himself and puts his clothes on. They get into a car, and head into Kyoto.

Miyako inspects the boat and the bird as they travel.

His dad glances at them.

"Origami," he says. "And not very good."

"And very wet," says Miyako, as the boat collapses between his fingers. He opens it and finds the blotchy faded words inside. He learns English at school, but most of this has seeped into the paper and is pretty meaningless. All he can decipher are the letters that make 'name', 'Mina' and 'ever'.

He finds the message in the bird as well.

"Mina again," he says.

He refolds the bird and flies it through the
tiny spaces around him.

"Careful," says his dad. "Don't block my view."

The streets are packed, the roads are so busy, the traffic's so slow. Dad keeps looking at his watch.

"We'll be late," he says. "She'll think we've forgotten about her."

"Hardly!" says Miyako.

He thinks of the one who wrote the messages. English, maybe. And probably a girl. He flies the bird before his eyes, and it's as if he can still feel the vibrations of its maker within it. He thinks of the girl, and an image of her starts to appear in his mind.

They don't really know it, of course, but as they
get close to the centre of Kyoto they slowly pass
Mina and her mum, who are standing at a tiny
temple that's squashed in between a shoe shop and
a bank. They've just rung a bell that hangs from the
temple eaves. They've enjoyed opening the paper
fortunes that tell them what their lucky numbers are.

Mina throws a coin into a small stone pond of
golden fish. Miyako watches her. There's something
familiar in the way she moves, the way she bows
her head. He continues to fly the bird.

r

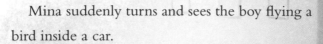

Mina suddenly turns and sees the boy flying a
bird inside a car.

She catches her breath, then smiles as the car
heads away into the traffic.

"Everybody makes them," she says.

Soon Miyako's dad drives underground, into a huge downward-spiralling car park. They're down at Level 6 before they find a space. Then they hurry to the escalators that zigzag through a huge department store towards the sky.

Sakura's at a table in the open roof café. She has a pot of coffee with two cups, and a glass of lemonade. She stands when she sees them, bows and smiles. Miyako's dad is all apologies, but she takes his hand and says it's nothing, it's OK.

"Good morning, Miyako," she says. "You have been in the water today?"

"Yes," he says.

She indicates the lemonade.

"For you," she says.

He thanks her. They're still awkward with each other. Miyako plays with the bird as she and his dad talk and laugh about some mysterious theatre they saw together.

Miyako unfolds the bird and writes his name beside the name of Mina.

He makes the bird again, then slips away from the table and goes to the parapet. He looks back. Sakura's OK, he supposes. His dad's laughing again. Change is coming, he knows that.

Miyako looks down over beautiful Kyoto: the crowded streets, the skyscrapers, the flashing lights, the gardens. He sees Kinkaku-ji itself. He's even sure he can see its reflection in the water.

He holds the bird above the parapet and flicks his wrist and lets it fly.

Mina and her mum walk happily hand-in-hand. Mina's imagining, as she often does, that her dad is walking beside her, too. Mum's bought a print of Mount Fuji rising from the mist. Mina's bought some manga, two versions of the same story contained within one book. The English version starts from the left, the Japanese from the right. The versions end and come together at the centre.

Mina and her mum love the crowds, the shops, the buses, the food, the temples. They love the silence and stillness at the heart of it all. It's the last day. Tomorrow it's a bullet train to Hiroshima. But they feel that even when they've left this place they'll still be here.

Mina looks up as they walk and here's the bird, swaying, falling, spinning, flying, a single tiny bird in all that space, a single tiny bird in space that goes on forever, as far as distant England, as far as the furthest star.

Mina raises her hands and the points of the bird touch the points of her fingers. She neatly folds her hands around it, then opens them, and shows it resting there.

"It can't be," says her mum.

But it is. Mina opens the bird, and there's her name, with the new unreadable beautiful word by its side.

They look up into the emptiness. There's nothing they can say.

They walk on through indecipherable Kyoto.

Miyako and his dad and Sakura come down on the zigzag escalators. Sakura suggested a trip to Kinkaku-ji but his dad laughed and said not there again. So they're heading for McDonald's and the cinema. Miyako knows they're doing it for him. That's OK. He's starting to feel at ease with her. He's even starting to like her, and to feel happy for his dad.

They walk through the sea of people. They come to the great pedestrian crossing where they wait for the lights to change and the traffic to stop. Mina and her mum are waiting at the far side.

The moment comes and the tides of people flow towards each other in the crowded city beneath the empty sky.

Mina and Miyako see each other.

They stop, and bring the adults who are with them to a stop as well.

"Konnichiwa!" says Miyako.

"Kon-ni-chi-wa!" says Mina.

AFTERWORD

David Almond

This story started on a bus in Tokyo. The bus was packed and we were standing. Outside were crowded pavements, busy traffic, shrines, noodle bars, pachinko parlours, flashing signs, skyscrapers, huge billboards. The bus moved and stopped, moved and stopped. A woman sat quietly by the bus window nearby. She had her head bowed as she worked with squares of paper, folding and refolding, making beasts and boats and birds. I was with my seven-year-old daughter, Freya, She was entranced. The woman saw us watching. She caught our eyes and nodded and smiled and went back to her work.

Then she looked up, reached out, and placed a paper boat in Freya's hands.

"Arigato," we said softly. Thank you.

The woman stood up, smiled and bowed, and left the bus and disappeared into the crowds.

We looked at the perfectly made gift in wonder. It was a moment that we'd remember for ever more. I never thought, of course, that it would lead to a story called *Paper Boat, Paper Bird*. But the ways of stories are mysterious. When I started to write it down much later, it felt as if it had always been there, that it had been given into my hands.

That was my first trip to Japan. It was springtime, cherry blossom time. I worked for a week in a school in Yokohama, then we travelled and wandered. We rode on the bullet train past Mount Fuji. We visited tiny streetside shrines and great temples with their gates in the sea. We went to see theatre – Kabuki, the drama so vigorous and bright, filled with vivid tales of battles and beheadings. We saw Noh drama at dusk in a temple garden, where ghosts emerged from darkness into subdued light, where the voices were so strange, the movement so slow, the music so haunting, as if coming from another world. We ate astonishing food, stocked up on exquisite Japanese stationery. We went to Kinkakuji in Kyoto, the famous temple that floats above its own reflection in the lake below.

We fell in love with Japan. All the way, without knowing it, I gathered details for the story that I'd come to write. All the way, we took that paper boat with us, and we brought it home with us.

Next time I went, my play of *Skellig* was about to

be produced in Tokyo. I met the cast. Skellig was to be played by a dancer. As I watched rehearsals, I sensed weird links between Skellig and the ghosts in Noh drama, which move slowly from darkness into light. It was so strange, so wonderful. Here were Skellig and Michael about come to life in Japan, so far from Newcastle, my home city, where the story was originally set. Here was Mina, talking in Japanese about William Blake and birds and joy and the need to be free.

I went again. This time I was invited by Professor Atsuko Hayakawa to work for a week at Tsuda University, which had been the first institution of higher education for women in Japan. Some of the students were writing theses on my work. I loved being there, talking with young people about writing and books and plays, experiencing the truth that stories draw us all together despite frontiers, different languages, different histories. Stories unite us, as all art does. Stories are acts of optimism and hope. They work against the forces of destruction.

On this visit, I had one of the most extraordinary encounters of my life. The Empress of Japan, Michiko, had invited me to the palace. Meet an empress? How would that be? Wouldn't it all be really difficult, really formal? Would we be able to talk properly to each other? Of course I knew I had to meet her too.

Atsuko's son, Yusuke, drove us to the palace. We drove through the traffic, the crowds, then through the palace gates and peaceful grounds. There was no ceremony, no formality. A smiling palace guard led us to a small, pale, quiet room. Beyond a wide window, there was a little garden nearby. We sat down and then the Empress came in. She wore a simple dress. She smiled and shook my hand warmly. She sat close by me and said how pleased she was. Her voice was soft and kind. A tray of tea and cakes was brought to us. The Empress talked about my work. She said how she loved *Skellig*. She talked about other books she loves. She writes poetry and tales herself. She has translated writings from other lands into Japanese. We talked together about the importance of children's books. In her beautiful speech to the 26th Congress of the International Board of Books for Young People (IBBY) she said,

"Sometimes a book can give a child the root of stability and security. Other times it seems a book gives wings to soar and fly just anywhere."

Yes. Books help us to feel safe and help us to be free.

I relaxed, of course, in the presence of this intelligent and kind woman. She talked about the beauty of the world, about disasters in her own land – war, earthquakes, the recent tsunami at Fukushima. She talked openly about her own life. I told her a little about the experiences behind some of my books. This was all so strange, so wonderful, so very unexpected. I felt so close to her, to this Empress.

At one point she sighed, and she nodded towards the garden past the window.

"I would like it to be wilder," she said, "just as Mina would."

I laughed.

"Yes. She would."

And then she said,

"I feel like Mina, David."

I caught my breath. I've heard so many people say this, children and adults from all walks of life, in the UK and all around the world. I feel like Mina. Now it was being said by the Empress, Michiko, here at the heart of Japan. Perhaps we both felt that Mina was in that room with us, too.

I was there for an hour, then we had to leave.

We drove back into the bustling metropolis.

I took her words and her voice and the memory with me. I took them back home to England with me.

Perhaps it was inevitable that I'd write a new story about Mina, in which she travels to Japan. In the tale, she doesn't go to the Palace. Like my daughter, Freya, she's on a crowded bus. A silent woman sits by the window, making origami boats and beasts and birds. She sees Mina watching and she smiles. And she places a beautifully folded paper boat into her hands.

"Arigato," says Mina. Thank you.

And so the story starts.

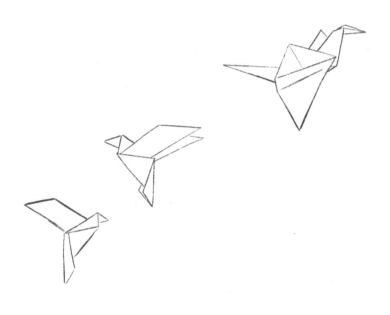

David Almond is the author of *Skellig*, *My Name is Mina*, *Heaven Eyes*, *Kit's Wilderness*, *A Song for Ella Grey* and many other novels, stories, picture books, opera librettos, songs and plays. His major awards include the Carnegie Medal, two Whitbread Awards, the Eleanor Farjeon Award and the Guardian Children's Fiction Prize. In 2010, he won the Hans Christian Andersen Award, the world's most prestigious prize for children's authors.

He lives in Newcastle, the city in which he was born.

In 2021, David was awarded an OBE for services to literature.

Kirsti Beautyman is an illustrator and children's book author based in Newcastle upon Tyne. You'll often find her in her small cosy studio, with her feet on a portable radiator, clutching a mug of hot Ribena while she works on her latest projects.

She graduated from Edinburgh College of Art in 2016 and was awarded 'Picture Hooks Illustrator of the Year' in 2017. Recently Kirsti has turned to working digitally, but her illustrations still always begin as a loose pencil sketch in one of many battered sketchbooks.

Read an extract from *SKELLIG*,
where we first met Mina

One

I found him in the garage on a Sunday afternoon. It was the day after we moved into Falconer Road. The winter was ending. Mum had said we'd be moving just in time for the spring. Nobody else was there. Just me. The others were inside the house with Doctor Death, worrying about the baby.

He was lying there in the darkness behind the tea chests, in the dust and dirt. It was as if he'd been there forever. He was filthy and pale and dried out and I thought he was dead. I couldn't have been more wrong. I'd soon begin to see the truth about him, that there'd never been another creature like him in the world.

We called it the garage because that's what the estate agent, Mr Stone, called it. It was more like a demolition site or a rubbish dump or like one of those ancient warehouses they keep pulling down at the quay. Stone led us down the garden, tugged the door open and shone his little torch into the gloom. We shoved our heads in at the doorway with him.

'You have to see it with your mind's eye,' he said. 'See it cleaned, with new doors and the roof repaired. See it as a wonderful two-car garage.'

He looked at me with a stupid grin on his face.

'Or something for you, lad – a hideaway for you and your mates. What about that, eh?'

I looked away. I didn't want anything to do with him. All the way round the house it had been the same. Just see it in your mind's eye. Just imagine what could be done. All the way round I kept thinking of the old man, Ernie Myers, that had lived here on his own for years. He'd been dead nearly a week before they found him under the table in the kitchen. That's what I saw when Stone told us about seeing with the mind's eye. He even said it when we got to the dining room and there was an old cracked toilet sitting there in the corner behind a plywood screen. I just wanted him to shut up, but he whispered that towards the end Ernie couldn't manage the stairs. His bed was brought in here and a toilet was put in so everything was easy for him. Stone looked at me like he didn't think I should know about such things. I wanted to get out, to get back to our old house again, but Mum and Dad took it all in. They went on like it was going to be some big adventure. They bought the house. They started cleaning it and scrubbing it and painting it. Then the baby came too early. And here we were.

Two

I nearly got into the garage that Sunday morning. I took my own torch and shone it in. The outside doors to the back lane must have fallen off years ago and there were dozens of massive planks nailed across the entrance. The timbers holding the roof were rotten and the roof was sagging in. The bits of the floor you could see between the rubbish were full of cracks and holes. The people that took the rubbish out of the house were supposed to take it out of the garage as well, but they took one look at the place and said they wouldn't go in it even for danger money. There were old chests of drawers and broken wash-basins and bags of cement, ancient doors leaning against the walls, deck chairs with the cloth seats rotted away. Great rolls of rope and cable hung from nails. Heaps of water pipes and great boxes of rusty nails were scattered on the floor. Everything was covered in dust and spiders' webs. There was mortar that had fallen from the walls. There was a little window in one of the walls but it was filthy and there were rolls of cracked lino standing in front of it. The place stank of rot and dust. Even the bricks were crumbling like they couldn't bear the weight any more. It was like the whole thing was sick of itself and would collapse in a heap and have to get bulldozed away.

I heard something scratching in one of the corners, and something scuttling about, then it all stopped and it was just dead quiet in there.

I stood daring myself to go in.

I was just going to slip inside when I heard Mum shouting at me.

'Michael! What you doing?'

She was at the back door.

'Didn't we tell you to wait till we're sure it's safe?'

I stepped back and looked at her.

'Well, didn't we?' she shouted.

'Yes,' I said.

'So keep out! All right?'

I shoved the door and it lurched half-shut on its single hinge.

'All right?' she yelled.

'All right.' I said. 'Yes. All right. All right.'

'Do you not think we've got more to worry about than stupid you getting crushed in a stupid garage?'

'Yes.'

'You just keep out, then! Right?'

'Right. Right, right, right.'

Then I went back into the wilderness we called a garden and she went back to the flaming baby.

Three

The garden was another place that was supposed to be wonderful. There were going to be benches and a table and a swing. There were going to be goalposts painted on one of the walls by the house. There was going to be a pond with fish and frogs in it. But there was none of that. There were just nettles and thistles and weeds and half-bricks and lumps of stone. I stood there kicking the heads off a million dandelions.

After a while, Mum shouted was I coming in for lunch and I said no, I was staying out in the garden. She brought me a sandwich and a can of Coke.

'Sorry it's all so rotten and we're all in such rotten moods,' she said.

She touched my arm.

'You understand, though. Don't you, Michael? Don't you?'

I shrugged.

'Yes,' I said.

She touched me again and sighed.

'It'll be great again when everything's sorted out,' she said.

I sat on a pile of bricks against the house wall. I ate the

sandwich and drank the Coke. I thought of Random Road where we'd come from, and all my old mates like Leakey and Coot. They'd be up on the top field now, playing a match that'd last all day.

Then I heard the doorbell ringing, and heard Doctor Death coming in. I called him Doctor Death because his face was grey and there were black spots on his hands and he didn't know how to smile. I'd seen him lighting up a fag in his car one day as he drove away from our door. They told me to call him Doctor Dan, and I did when I had to speak to him, but inside he was Doctor Death to me, and it fitted him much better.

I finished the Coke, waited a minute, then I went down to the garage again. I didn't have time to dare myself or to stand there listening to the scratching. I switched the torch on, took a deep breath, and tiptoed straight inside.

Something little and black scuttled across the floor. The door creaked and cracked for a moment before it was still. Dust poured through the torch beam. Something scratched and scratched in a corner. I tiptoed further in and felt spider webs breaking on my brow. Everything was packed in tight – ancient furniture, kitchen units, rolled-up carpets, pipes and crates and planks. I kept ducking down under the hosepipes and ropes and kitbags that hung from the roof. More cobwebs snapped on my clothes and skin. The floor was broken and crumbly. I opened a cupboard an inch, shone the torch in and saw a million woodlice scattering away. I peered down into a great stone jar and saw the bones of some little animal that had died in there. Dead bluebottles were everywhere. There were ancient newspapers and magazines. I shone the torch on to one and saw that it came from nearly fifty years ago. I moved so carefully. I was scared every moment that the whole thing was going to collapse. There was dust clogging my throat and nose. I knew they'd be yelling for me soon and I knew I'd better get out. I leaned across a heap of tea chests and shone the torch into the space behind and that's when I saw him.

I thought he was dead. He was sitting with his legs stretched out, and his head tipped back against the wall. He was covered in dust and webs like everything else and his face was thin and pale. Dead bluebottles were scattered on his hair and shoulders. I shone the torch on his white face and his black suit.

'What do you want?' he said.

He opened his eyes and looked up at me.

His voice squeaked like he hadn't used it in years.

'What do you want?'

My heart thudded and thundered.

'I said, what do you want?'

Then I heard them yelling for me from the house.

'Michael! Michael! Michael!'

I shuffled out again. I backed out through the door.

It was Dad. He came down the path to me.

'Didn't we tell you—' he started.

'Yes,' I said. 'Yes. Yes.'

I started to brush the dust off myself. A spider dropped away from my chin on a long string.

He put his arm around me.

'It's for your own good,' he said.

He picked a dead bluebottle out of my hair.

He thumped the side of the garage and the whole thing shuddered.

'See?' he said. 'Imagine what might happen.'

I grabbed his arm to stop him thumping it again.

'Don't,' I said. 'It's all right. I understand.'

He squeezed my shoulder and said everything would be better soon.

He laughed.

'Get all that dust off before your mother sees, eh?'